THE SINISTER SUBSTITUTE

By Preeti Chhibber

Illustrated by James Lancett

Scholastic Inc.

ISBN 978-1-338-58719-7

1 2020

Printed in the U.S.A.   23
First printing 2021

Book design by Katie Fitch

CHAPTER 1

Yesterday! Was! Great!!!

Miles, Kamala, Evan, Tippy-Toe, and I are trying to get in as many Fun-Time Hang-Out sessions as we can before Avengers Institute starts again. I've already started today's scrapbook!

☑ Went to Luna Park on Coney Island and

☑ Ate too many hot dogs

MUNCH! MUNCH!

☑ Followed by too much ice cream

LICK!

☑ Rode the Wonder Wheel, the Cyclone, and the Thunderbolt

☑ Waited for Evan outside the bathrooms after the Thunderbolt

BLERRGH!

☑ Defeated a group of super villains who attacked the park

☑ Watched the fireworks

DOREEN'S NOTES

So, new year . . . Don't get me wrong, I think we're all excited to get back to class and learn some new stuff . . . or at least, me and Evan are definitely excited. Miles and Kamala are freaking out a bit because this semester is the science fair and they want to do a good job. But they're so good! I know they'll do an amazing job! I did the fair last semester and it was so easy—I created the code for a little robot squirrel and it was the <u>cutest</u>.

WHAT DO ALL THESE HEROES HAVE IN COMMON?

SCIENCE!

IT'S TIME FOR THE
AVENGERS INSTITUTE
SCIENCE FAIR!

DOREEN'S NOTES

Anyway, we've been keeping the streets safe, no ifs, ands, or nuts about it. Sometimes that means team-building exercises! Today I got to pick the exercise and I called on a very special friend . . .

I feel like maybe I'm forgetting something? Like, there's something I'm supposed to be doing right this moment that I've totally forgot? Hmm . . .

8

9

MS. QUIZZLER'S NOTES FOR THE ULTIMATE QUIZZLER QUIZ SHOW

What do you call a lonely banana?

Ans: Akela

Note: Origin, Hindi. Akela means "alone," and the word <u>kela</u> means "banana."

What's a cat's favorite color?

Ans: Purrrple

Note: This isn't accurate, but Squirrel Girl taught me the joy of wordplay!

What is a thirsty man's favorite question?

Ans: Who?

Note: The chemical composition of water is H_2O: H-OO.

What do you call a cowardly octopus?

Ans: Spineless

Note: The octopus is one of nature's most well-known invertebrates.

From the desk of Dr. Bruce Banner

Avengers Assembly, it's time to SCIENCE!

Get ready to . . .

**Have an awesome, science-filled time!
Use scientific equipment properly!
Learn how to invent
and experiment safely!
Know when to stop!**

**I know what you're thinking, but I only
have this to say:**

Radiate? More like RADI-GREAT!

Voice Mail

▶

Voice-mail transcript from MOM

"Hi Dor—Squirrel Girl! Sorry, peanut, I know you want us to use your code name more often. Just calling to check in and see where you are— hopefully not involved in any of the fighting nonsense down at Coney Island. I thought I saw a squirrel tail on the news, but I'm sure I was mistaken because you promised you were just going to hang out with friends. Anyway, call me back. Love you! This is Mom."

Voice-mail transcript from NANCY "BIFFLE CAKES" WHITEHEAD

"Hey, are we still on to hang later? I, uh, caught a bit of the Coney Island news. Let me know if you wanna reschedule."

CHAPTER 2

IS YOUR MIDDLE NAME NOT SQUIRREL GIRL?

NANCY! YOU KNOW THAT'S NOT TRUE. AND ALSO, I AM SORRY I'M NOT THERE, FRIEND! TODAY GOT AWAY FROM ME AND I . . . PECAN'T CATCH UP.

YOUR MOM?? IS EVERYTHING OKAY?? DID SOMEONE TRY TO KIDNAP YOUR PARENTS AGAIN?!

NO, NO! THEY'RE FINE. MY MOM JUST HAD **ANOTHER** COMMENT ABOUT ME DOING THE SUPER HERO THING. IT'S BEEN HAPPENING ALL BREAK. SHE AND MY DAD ARE WORRIED THAT I'M NOT DOING ENOUGH KID STUFF, BUT . . . I AM! WE ATE HOT DOGS TODAY! WHAT'S MORE KID THAN THAT?! HOT DOGS, I TELL YOU!

OKAY, YOU'RE RIGHT. THE WORLD DEFINITELY NEEDS SQUIRREL GIRL—IMAGINE IF YOU HADN'T HELPED AT CONEY ISLAND TODAY AND ALL THOSE PEOPLE WHO WOULD'VE BEEN HURT, BUT—WELL, WAIT, I SEE YOU.

I SEE YOU, TOO!

DOREEN'S NOTES

Okay, had a much-needed hangout with Biffle Cakes today. I didn't realize how long it had been since we'd gotten to spend some time one-on-one and in real life! . . . But Nancy did what Nancy does best and put it to me straight.

I was telling her I was worried about how much my parents don't want me to be super-heroing, and well, it went something like this:

Me: I'm just worried about going back to the institute with this stuff at home. My mom left me a voice mail of guilt! A guilt mail.

Nancy: You know they won't stop you from going to school. They love you! And like I said, You definitely should not give up being Squirrel Girl. What do your parents think is a better career considering the T-A-I-L?

DOREEN'S NOTES

Tippy-Toe: Chirruk chirruk.

Me: She's asking why you're spelling "tail."

Nancy: . . . It was a joke, Tippy-Toe.

Tippy-Toe: Chirruk chirruk chirruk.

Me: She says it wasn't very funny.

Nancy: Well, maybe you're not very funny,
Tippy-Toe. Anyway, you're definitely meant to
be a super hero! Buuuuuuuuuuuuuut . . .

Me: Nuts! But what?

Nancy: But, well, look at these.

NUTWORK

Monday 5:15 PM

NANCY: Hey! ????

DOREEN: Sry! am fghtng evilllll rn!!

Tuesday 6:34 PM

NANCY: Still on to go over that coding block for class?

DOREEN: AH! I totally forgot I had to patrol 2night. Sorry!! 😔

NANCY: . . .

NUTWORK

Wednesday 8:30 PM

NANCY: Plan: CAT GODS 3 on Friday. I got tix, then sleepover at urs, and then waffle breakfast—yes, I will put walnuts on yours.

DOREEN: Pls don't hate me, but I have to do a team-up on Friday to take down this guy who is stealing ppl's laundry money—the Clean Sheet.

Today 4:15 PM

NANCY: I'm guessing since you're not here that you are doing after-school stuff but we were supposed to get mochas! And I'm here! Alone!!!!!

DOREEN:

DOREEN'S NOTES

Basically, Nancy doesn't agree with my parents, but she brought up some good points. Like, I'm being kind of a jerk who has been ignoring her best friend <u>way</u> too much (my words, not hers). But I am going to be better about it! One thing that's important to learn is how to balance being a hero and being a regular person—ooh, maybe that will be one of our classes this year! That would be convenient.

Tippy-Toe thinks I just need to be better at scheduling my time and writing things down in my planner. I reminded Tippy that I am pretty good at that part, but super villains don't always ask about my schedule before deciding to break the law.

Anyway, if I can get through defeating a secret plot against a teammate <u>and</u> come out of the first semester with new best friends, I think I can handle being a full-time student and being a super hero! This is <u>my year!</u>

TO: Kamala Khan <k-khan2014@heatmail.com>; Doreen Green <acornluvr@heatmail.com>; Evan Sabahnur <evan_sabahnur@heatmail.com>

FROM: Miles Morales <MilesMorales@heatmail.com>

Subject: Fwd: Welcome back, students

LOL "UNANTICIPATED ISSUES" AKA A WHOLE GROUP OF KIDS BUILT A WHOLE EVIL PLAN TRYIN' TO TAKE U DOWN, K!!!

Miles

TO: Avengers Institute Students <avengers-student-list-serv@avengers-institute.com>

FROM: Carol Danvers <cdanvers@avengers-institute.com>

Subject: Welcome back, students

Dear Students,

Welcome to another semester at Avengers Institute. We're excited to announce some changes to the institute in light of the unanticipated issues of last semester. We've brought on a few new teachers and instead of only a few independent studies, this semester every student will now be enrolled in one so as to foster a more direct connection between our professors and the student population.

You'll be hearing more about your schedule and independent study selection from Vice Principal Maximoff in the next few days. For now, let me say that I am proud of the work you all did last semester and I'm looking forward to seeing you all again.

Col. Carol Danvers
Principal, Avengers Institute

* Translated from squirrel-ese — "You said it!"

* Translated from squirrel-ese — "Your friends are right there!"

*Translated from squirrel-ese — "SQUIRRELS ARE NOT CHIPMUNKS, YOU TRASH PANDA!"

CHAPTER 3

SQUIRREL GIRL'S AVENGERS INSTITUTE CLASS SCHEDULE

TO: Doreen Green <acornluvr@heatmail.com>

FROM: Pietro Maximoff
<pmaximoff@avengers-institute.com>

Subject: Class Schedule

Hello Ms. Green,

Please find your class schedule pasted below. Note that thanks to a pranking Asgardian, we are contractually obligated to refer to Professor Thor as Protector of Midgard; however, as a student, you are not bound by such rules, so you can call him whatever you want. Please take advantage.

Best,
Pietro Maximoff
Vice Principal, Avengers Institute

MONDAY: TOOLS OF THE SUPER HERO TRADE with Professor Thor Odinson, Protector of Midgard

I wonder if we'll get to try and hold Mjolnir!!

Tuesday: ETHICS AND YOU with Professor Jennifer Walters, Esquire

Remember to ask Professor Walters about Squirrel Working Hours.

Wednesday: INTERDIMENSIONAL TRAVEL & DIPLOMACY with Professor Lockjaw

!!! Kamala had so much fun in her I-T class last semester. I hope we get to go visit the Atlanteans again!

Thursday: THE ACTION SEQUENCE with visiting professors Rocket and Groot

Okay, this will be fine. It will be fun. They'll love me!

Friday: INDEPENDENT STUDY with Professor Scott Lang

Will I get to be a TINY SQUIRREL GIRL???

DOREEN'S NOTES

Proof I have the <u>best</u> schedule. Let's start with our first class with Professor Thor because it was one heck of a <u>Macademic</u> experience! (But also, it was a little weird. We'll get to that.) Anyway, Professor sent us a list ahead of time of things to bring to the class, but I don't think I was alone in having trouble finding them all . . .

1. "Any hammer you have at home, young heroes." Easy enough! I'll bring my whole toolbox! It's shaped like an acorn. :D

2. "An axe." Are . . . we allowed to own axes in New York?

DOREEN'S NOTES

3. "Any <u>magic</u> tools obtained as <u>spoils</u> of war." I need to get spoils from my next battle, omigosh.

4. "Armor, You will need armor, but if You haven't any, worry not! We will pay a visit to the Blacksmith of the Gods!" I cannot wait to tell Nancy we might get to go to ASGARD and get matching armor for me and Tippy-Toe. She will freak. Out.

5. "The hopes and dreams of your family! Your legacies!" Erm . . .

EVAN: That was strange, right?

DOREEN: Yeah, SUPER STRANGE! Did anyone recognize the voice? Or see where it came from?

MILES: Nah, and I know everyone—that didn't sound like anyone at our school.

EVAN: Nova and Amadeus were talking about it and Nova thinks that it's Ant-Man pranking Thor.

KAMALA: . . .

DOREEN: Ha ha, do you think so, K?

KAMALA: I mean, I guess I wouldn't not believe it was Professor Lang.

MILES: What?

FILE NAME: ETHICS AND YOU
PROFESSOR JENNIFER WALTERS, ESQUIRE

PROCEDURAL HISTORY: Students have returned for their
second semester of Avengers Institute. We're moving on to the
advanced notion of ethical dilemmas as they pertain to super
heroing.

ISSUE: How many versions of "right" are there?

A TRANSCRIPT OF OPENING REMARKS

JENNIFER WALTERS, ESQUIRE AKA SHE-HULK: Hello, class.
Welcome back. I'm still Professor Walters, but this semester is
going to be a LOT more work, so don't get too comfortable. We
are going to talk about legalities and philosophy and—

DOREEN GREEN AKA SQUIRREL GIRL: I am SO EXCITED to be
back, Professor Walters!

SHE-HULK: Thank you, Squirrel Girl. Now, as I was saying—

SAM ALEXANDER AKA NOVA: Professor? Can I ask a legal
question?

SHE-HULK: [pause] Yes, Nova.

NOVA: Say that while someone was flying—not me, but some
hypothetical flying person—while this hypothetical person was
flying, they flew through the New York City Marathon and
maybe ruined a few people's marathon times, could they, uh,
be sued for that?

SHE-HULK: What?

SQUIRREL GIRL: But you were just trying to stop that guy from stealing that lady's purse, Nova! No one will want to sue you.

TIPPY-TOE [a squirrel]: Chirruk chirruk! Chirruk?

SQUIRREL GIRL: He's not getting sued, Tippy-Toe! I don't think he'll give you his helmet, even if he does go to jail.

NOVA: [let the record show Nova's voice is an octave higher than normal] It wasn't me! Hypothetical! Hypothetical!

KAMALA KHAN AKA MS. MARVEL: [whispering to MILES MORALES AKA SPIDER-MAN] I saw that online. Nova ate it right in front of the finish line and caused a huge pileup.

SPIDER-MAN: [whispering back] I took a screenshot; it was my phone background for weeks.

SHE-HULK: Nova, we can discuss this after class, but—never mind, after class. See me after class. [pause] Okay, I hope you all brought your books because we're starting with Plato.

AMADEUS CHO AKA BRAWN: Professor, I wonder if we could spend time debating who gets to say what is right? Why do "heroes" get to decide? Would "villains" be right if they won more battles?

SHE-HULK: . . . That's an interesting question, Amadeus. And another one we can discuss after class.

DOREEN'S NOTES

Another weird class! Professor Walters looked really put out by Amadeus's question, though I'm not sure I understand why. He was supposed to stay after class, but I think Nova tired the professor out and so she told Amadeus to come back later.

. . . But do you want to know the weirdest thing?

I saw him in the hallway right before I was coming home, and I asked him what that question meant . . . but he had no idea what I was talking about! And Amadeus usually remembers everything.

Tippy-Toe thinks he was just messing with me to be funny, but I don't know.

At least tomorrow is our first day of a new semester's Interdimensional Travel class! I wonder where Professor Lockjaw is taking us *this time*.

41

DOREEN'S NOTES

Miles and I were <u>lucky</u> to get back to school in one piece! Professor Lockjaw dropped us in the class and immediately teleported somewhere else—probably to talk to the rest of the Fantastic Four to see what was going on. Miles texted Spider-Man to ask, so hopefully we'll know more soon!

. . . Of course this could all be an elaborate teaching exercise to keep us on our toes? If something happens in tomorrow's class, I am going to be <u>veeeeery</u> suspicious.

. . . Tippy-Toe says I should be suspicious now, but no one else seems squicked out by what's going on, so I'm going to wait.

MILES: 🤚 is there any reason that we should be avoiding the F4 bc I think the rock dude was trying to capture me and Squirrel Girl yesterday

THE OTHER SPIDER-MAN: Welcome to the wide, wide world of super heroing, kid!

MILES: ??

THE OTHER SPIDER-MAN: Jokes! I'll ask around but for now, def let Carol know.

MILES: Lockjaw was there!

THE OTHER SPIDER-MAN: Oh, it was probably just a test. I'll double check, but my guess is that it was a way to remind you to pay attention to everyone, no matter what suit they have on.

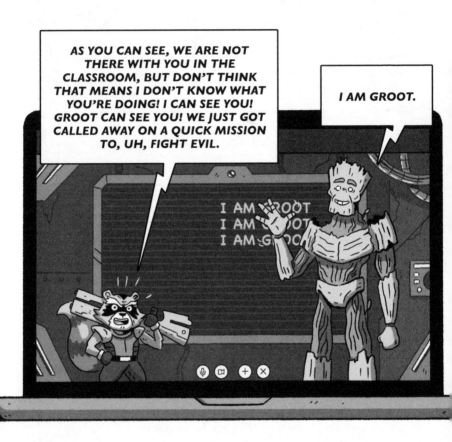

CHATBOX:

AMERICA: Is Professor Groot saying we can leave early? I think that means we can leave early.

EVAN: . . . I guess it could mean that.

MS. MARVEL: That one *definitely* meant we're the best students they've ever had! 😆

SQUIRREL GIRL: Is there a class for learning Groot?

NOVA: I speak Groot, and Ms. Marvel is right. Definitely. We are not making this up at all.

I AM GROOT.

YOU'RE ALL THE WORST. GROOT, STOP ENCOURAGING THEM. WE HAVE TO TEACH THEM ABOUT HOW TO FIGHT GOOD.

CHATBOX:

AMERICA: I can punch a star-shaped hole in reality, Professor Rocket.

CHATBOX:

MS. MARVEL: Professor Rocket, one quick question, what do the one to three "I am Groots" mean on the board behind you?

DOREEN'S NOTES

I have no idea if that was a normal or a weird class . . . but Tippy-Toe says she asked around the squirrel community, and it was normal for Rocket and Groot.

. . . Gotta remember to ask Tippy-Toe why the squirrels know so much about Rocket and Groot.

Tomorrow's the last day of my first week and it's just me and Professor Lang! I asked Kamala what he was like and she said he's "not the most professional professor but he definitely cares." She's pretty sure he didn't get that maze we did in the decathlon approved before he did it, for example.

Also, he tells really bad jokes! I'm going to use all the nut puns I want!

I am going to go nuts with puns. I'm about to meet Miles to help him with this science fair thing so I can try some of these out . . .

NAME OF CLASS: Independent Study with Squirrel Girl

NOTE TO SELF: Send Hank McCoy an email to say thanks for giving me his lesson plan template—it is a GAME CHANGER.

PROFESSOR: Professor Scott Lang

(LOOK AT ME, MA, I'M A PROFESSOR!)

OVERVIEW: Why am I teaching _this_ class? Oh, wait, what did Carol say? Oh right, we are going to work on being better mentors . . .

OBJECTIVE: Uh, what I said up there.

NOTES:

You can do this, Scott! You're a great teacher! You've got th——

CHAPTER 4

TO: Pietro Maximoff <pmaximoff@avengers-institute.com>

FROM: Scott Lang <ant-man@avengers-institute.com>

Subject: Weird thing

Heyyyyy Maximan—do you know what this is? It was on my desk and I have no idea where it came from. Or what it means? I sent it to Carol, but I got her Out of Office reply. Where is she?

Also, uh, I don't know if I taught my last class. I do not *remember anything*. Granted, I didn't sleep at all last night—up late doing Avenger stuff, but uh, that's not important.

ANYWAY, seems like something you should know about. Could just be a prank, but after last semester . . . IDK, figured I'd send it your way.

Scott

ATTACHMENT:

Operation T D S H S

1. Break trust
2. Divide
3. Encourage rivalries
4. Bask in chaos

ATTACHED: weirdthing.jpg

TO: Scott Lang <ant-man@avengers-institute.com>

**FROM: Pietro Maximoff
<pmaximoff@avengers-institute.com>**

Subject: RE: Weird thing

Scott,

1—I stopped reading after you called me Maximan because I have explicitly asked you not to call me that at least seventeen times.

2—You're lucky I opened an email called "weird thing" at all.

Pietro

ATTACHMENT:

ATTACHED: STOP.jpg

NOVA

FLIP!

Scenes from our first week!

QUICKSILVER

And he never even noticed. 😂

In which we kick the butts of the boys!

CHAPTER 5

Hey, guys! I gotta talk to you all about something.

Hey, Doreen! Any chance this can be quick? Miles and I are SO BEHIND on this project.

Uh, yeah, sorry, Doreen! . . . We are, uh—Kamala, this might be about to explode, but I'm not sure.

Er, yeah, I second keeping it quick. I forgot to write that ethics essay and it's due tomorrow.

Okay, I-think-that-something-fishy-is-going-on-at-school-because-I-saw-Rocket-and-Vice-Principal Maximoff-fighting-in-the-hall-and-that-thing-with-Nova-and-also-why-are-so-many-people-lying-it's-weird-there-is-definitely-something-going-on!

Okay, one more time, but maybe not *that* quick.

I saw the vice principal and Professor Rocket in the hall arguing about how Rocket gave us bad advice—

Rocket *does* give us bad advice.

But what about the Nova thing! He didn't tell *us* that.

So, he told it to him after class? AH! K, I think I broke something.

Ah, sorry, Doreen! We gotta go, but it does sound like maybe this is just Professor Rocket being weird?

Wait—oh, they're gone.

A TRANSCRIPT OF MS. MARVEL AND SPIDER-MAN
TRYING TO BUILD AN ACTUAL VOLCANO

NOTE: No, not one of those volcanoes you get in the
average science fair. This is a miniature version of a
real volcano. Magma and all.

SETTING: An empty lab at Avengers Institute. There is
definitely an unattended shrink ray in the corner.

THE PLAYERS:

MS. MARVEL

SPIDER-MAN

AMADEUS CHO (AKA BRAWN)

AMERICA CHAVEZ

The desks in the room have been cleared to allow
students more space to work on their projects. MS.
MARVEL and SPIDER-MAN are in the back next to a
large mound of tightly packed dirt. They are surrounded
by papers and bottles. AMADEUS CHO and AMERICA
CHAVEZ are on the other side of the room. AMADEUS
is hammering against a massive metal monstrosity.
AMERICA is looking at her phone.

SCENE 1

MS. MARVEL: Okay, Spidey, we got special approval from Carol Danvers *herself* to use this chemical to make realistic magma, so we cannot mess this up. I will not disappoint my namesake.

SPIDER-MAN: Relax, Ms. M, we got this!

[SPIDER-MAN has spoken too soon, and an explosion rocks their area of the room]

AMERICA CHAVEZ: [starts to run forward to grab whoever she can] AH!

AMADEUS CHO: [getting ready to jump into a fire to save his classmates] Whoa! You guys okay back there?

MS. MARVEL: [coughing] Yeah [cough], we're okay [cough].

SPIDER-MAN: Yeah, we're okay! Sorry about that! I, uh—

MS. MARVEL: [glaring at Spider-Man] *Used too much of the chemical I just told you to be careful with?*

SPIDER-MAN: My bad, Ms. M.

[SPIDER-MAN realizes he needs to distract MS. MARVEL]

SPIDER-MAN: What are you two making for your project?

AMERICA: We're making a universal tracer, like, it'll find *anything* and *anywhere*. It was my idea. The last time I punched through dimensions I left my phone somewhere and I had to get a new one.

AMADEUS CHO: [back to hammering on their machine] It was a really good idea, and I think I can isolate fragments of reality or dimensions using this equation—

SPIDER-MAN: [making eye contact with MS. MARVEL to make sure they both know they need to stop AMADEUS before he really gets going] We're making a real, working tiny volcano.

MS. MARVEL: It's going to be SO CUTE.

AMERICA: That's cool—oh, is that why it exploded?

AMADEUS CHO: [staring at SPIDER-MAN and MS. MARVEL] DID PRINCIPAL COLONEL DANVERS GIVE YOU ACCESS TO—

MS. MARVEL: We are *not* allowed to discuss it! We gotta go!

SPIDER-MAN: [waves sheepishly]

Best Lab Partners Ever

SHAKE
SHAKE

SEVAN_06 Starting the day with a brain smoothie because I have so much homework to do 😔

Liked by MILES2MILLAS, AcornLuvr, and 3 others

SEVAN_06 ✌️

Liked by AcornLuvr, MILES2MILLAS, and 2 others

MILES2MILLAS Next time I'm joining! Gotta get those stretches in 💪

SEVAN_06 Just a #LaterShot celebrating friends

Liked by Slothbaby, MILES2MILLAS, and 3 others

AcornLuvr <3

MILES2MILLAS <3

Slothbaby <3

SEVAN_06 FINISHED MY ESSAY SO IT IS TIME FOR FACE! MASKS! AND! CARTOONS!

Liked by Slothbaby, AcornLuvr, and 3 others

Slothbaby Where is mine tho? 🫤

AcornLuvr Same ? ^^^

DOREEN'S NOTES

Everyone is too distracted! I know there is something sketchy going on at Avengers Institute. But if my own teammates won't listen to me, why would the teachers? UGH!

AND I got home and my mom was so mad that I was late for dinner, like there aren't more important things happening than dinner. She kept dropping hints about wanting me to quit the institute.

And it was so obvious. They're not even trying.

DOREEN'S NOTES

DOREEN: Mom, can you pass the walnut casserole?

MOM: You could casseROLE right out of that school if you wanted, and be home on time, peanut!

DAD: You know, Doreen . . . I think you might want to give up this super hero business. Be a regular kid again!

DOREEN'S NOTES

Why can't they understand that I can't leave my friends or stop helping people who need me, and that I love doing it!

. . . Speaking of which, Tippy-Toe thinks I should text Nancy, but she's so mad at me. I've been such an awful friend.

I feel terrible. Oh gosh.

I should just do it. I should just rip the Band-Aid off and do it!

DOREEN: First of all, I am the sorriest friend that ever there was. I have no excuse except that going to two schools all day is a lot of work, but I should have texted back! I am SO SORRY! I LOVE YOU! I don't want you to feel bad! Nancy! YOU ARE THE CASH TO MY SHEW! THE AL TO MY MOND! THE PISTACH TO MY IO!

NANCY: . . . . . .

NANCY: . . . . . .

NANCY: . . . . . .

NANCY: . . . . . .

NANCY: . . . . . .

NANCY: . . . . . .

NANCY: . . . . . .

NANCY: . . . . . .

NANCY: . . . . Okay that's a pretty good apology even though I am still mad.

NANCY: You can't just disappear! That's not fair!

DOREEN: You are 100% correct! I'll tell you about everything! Especially bc . . . I think something bad is happening at the institute.

NANCY: ????

DOREEN: Wanna video chat?

SO! WHAT'S HAPPENING??

OKAY, SO I'VE SEEN SOME WEIRD STUFF GOING ON WITH THE TEACHERS AND STUDENTS. THERE WAS A WEIRD, MYSTERIOUS VOICE IN MY FIRST CLASS WITH THOR THAT SEEMED LIKE IT WAS JUST TRYING TO THROW HIM OFF. THEN, ONE OF MY CLASSMATES ASKED A SUPER-WEIRD QUESTION IN MY ETHICS CLASS, SOMEONE WHO WOULD USUALLY NOT DO THAT— IT'S BRAWN, I CAN'T PRETEND—

PLEASE TELL ME EVERYTHING ABOUT THOR???? HE'S SO HANDSOME.

HE IS! BUT OKAY, THERE'S MORE. NOVA TOTALLY BLEW UP AT ME AND SPIDEY BECAUSE HE SAID ONE OF OUR TEACHERS—ROCKET RACOON—TOLD HIM THAT IF HE WAS TOO BUSY OR SOMETHING HE COULD WALK AWAY FROM A FIGHT?

ONE OF YOUR TEACHERS IS ROCKET RACCOON???? I THOUGHT HE STOLE STUFF FROM THE AVENGERS.

MAYBE THAT'S WHY HE OWES PRINCIPAL DANVERS A FAVOR? . . . HMM. ANYWAY, THEN, I SAW VICE PRINCIPAL MAXIMOFF AND ROCKET ARGUING IN THE HALLWAY ABOUT IT, BUT ROCKET SAID HE NEVER TOLD ANYONE TO DO THAT! PLUS, MY INDEPENDENT STUDY TEACHER, ANT-MAN, IS BEING REALLY CREEPY AND WEIRD AND TELLING ME THAT ALL THE STUFF WE LEARNED LAST SEMESTER AND SUPPORTING OUR TEAMMATES WAS WRONG.

WHAT DO YOUR TEAMMATES SAY?

WELL, THIS SEMESTER IS BONKERS! THEY'RE OVERLOADING US WITH HOMEWORK, SO EVERYONE IS DISTRACTED AND BUSY AND WE'RE ALL NOT CONNECTING LIKE WE WERE. I COULDN'T GET THEM TO FOCUS AND THEY ALL HAVE SO MUCH STUFF GOING ON, THEY DIDN'T EVEN HEAR ME.

MAN I KNOW HOW THAT FEELS. OKAY, HERE'S WHAT WE'RE GOING TO DO. I'M GOING TO DO SOME DIGGING AND SEE WHAT I CAN FIND OUT ABOUT ROCKET AND ANT-MAN AND THE SCHOOL AND SEE IF THERE'S ANYTHING WEIRD GOING ON ONLINE. IF IT EXISTS, IT'S PROBABLY ON THE INTERNET. GIVE ME A DAY OR TWO.

YOU ARE THE BEST AND A MILLION TIMES BETTER FRIEND THAN I AM AND I AM SORRY AGAIN AND NOW TELL ME ABOUT EVERYTHING IN YOUR LIFE!!!

CHAPTER 6

AvengersInstituteSecretsOut.moomblr.com

NOVA NEEDS TO GET THAT PAPER

tags: lol, oops, Nova

DOREEN: OMG! LOL! What is this??? Nova with toilet paper?

NANCY: Yeah . . . it starts funny but . . .

AvengersInstituteSecretsOut.moomblr.com

Amadeus Cho . . . the cheater???

Rumor has it that Amadeus Cho, supposedly super smart, cheated on his placement tests. Could this be true??

tags: yikes, liar, cheater

NUTWORK

DOREEN: I don't know, Nancy, thank you for finding it. But I don't know what this has to do with the stuff at school? This just seems mean. There are mean kids everywhere. I'll probably tell VPQS about it, tho.

NANCY: If you say so . . . I'll keep an eye on it, either way. Just in case.

DOREEN: Thank you! Let me know if you find anything. I'll keep you updated about weird stuff at school.

NANCY: Wait, you have class w/ Ant-Man today, right?

DOREEN: Yeah.

NANCY: Try to record it. If he's being weird, then I can see what you mean!

EmbiggenFeels.moomblr.com

AcornLuvr:
Hey! Have you seen this?
AvengersInstituteSecretsOut.
moomblr.com

Slothbaby:
What is this???

W3bbed4Life:
Uh no, is that Nova?? LOLLLL
WITH TOILET PAPER???

SEVAN_06:
This seems mean! Amadeus
wouldn't *cheat*.

Slothbaby:
Ant-Man would totally fall into
the trash, tho. 🤷🏽‍♀️

AcornLuvr:
I agree w/ Evan, I think it's
mean. I was gonna tell the VP.

Slothbaby:
You should! It is mean and could get even meaner real fast.
Even if that picture of Nova is pretty funny.

W3bbed4Life:
I'm saving it. He has that one of me saved where I had avocado on my mask and no one told me.

AcornLuvr:
lol that is a fair trade, Spidey. k I have indie study rn, but I'll go to the VP after!

SEVAN_06:
I think he already left campus today, but try tmrw!

AcornLuvr:
k thanx, Evan!

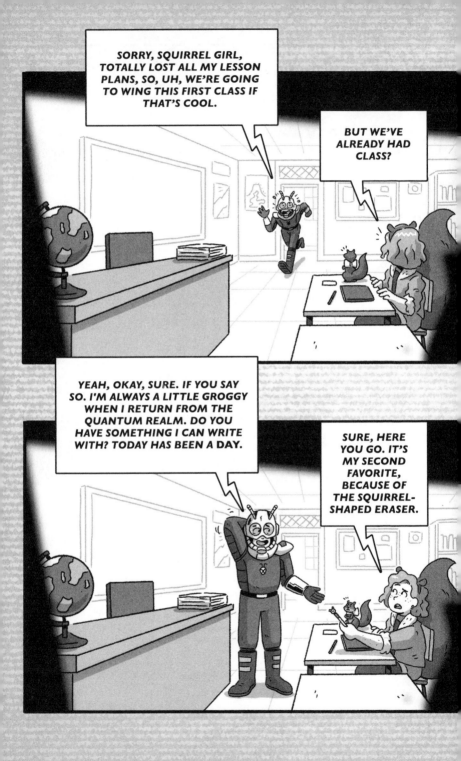

87

CHAPTER 7

AVENGERS IN

AVENGERS INSTITUTE'S HALLOWED HALLS VANDALIZED

In the deep negative space of our absence, someone trespassed our halls and messed their way through the school.

By the editorial board, approved by *Post* editor Ironheart

This afternoon, students entered Avengers Institute not to order, as they've come to expect, but chaos. The entry hall of our beloved school was covered in toilet paper, trash, and spray paint. We managed to get a few pictures before we were unceremoniously removed from the area by Vice Principal Maximoff, who only had this to say: "Please leave, you are in my way."

Who could have done this horrible thing? Where is our school pride?

Rumor is that Principal Danvers and Vice Principal Maximoff will be interviewing culprits later today, and don't you worry, the *Post* will be there to get the dirt!

Squirrel Girl and Amadeus Cho, please come to my office.

DOREEN'S NOTES

Today I got called to the principal's office and it was awful. Someone really trashed our school . . . and this is where I think all the weirdness has officially caught up with me. But let me start at the beginning.

After the auditorium, Amadeus and I went to Principal Danvers's office and it was very awkward. So obviously, I tried to break the ice!

Me: Hey, Amadeus, do you know . . . what's going on?

Amadeus: No idea. I hate not knowing things.

Me: Well, at least we're here together!

Amadeus: . . . Sure. Although unless you know something, I don't know how helpful that is.

DOREEN'S NOTES

Me: Solidarity? Misery loves company?

Then he gave me a weird look, but before he could say anything, he got called into Principal Danvers's office.

It was quiet for a while, and then there was a crash and Amadeus yelling,

"I AM TOO SMART TO CHEAT. ARE YOU KIDDING ME? OTHER THAN MOON GIRL, I'M PROBABLY THE SMARTEST PERSON HERE."

And then it was quiet again. A few minutes later he walked out the door and left without saying anything to me. But he seemed really upset.

Then it was my turn.

DOREEN'S NOTES

"Squirrel Girl? Could you come in here, please?"

When I walked in, Principal Danvers was there and Vice Principal Maximoff. They were both looking at me like I was the one who vandalized the school . . . because, well . . .

"Squirrel Girl, can you come look at this, please."

She gestured for me to look at the screen on her desk, and it was that same weird moomblr, the one Nancy showed me!

. . . Only now I was at the top!

DOREEN'S NOTES

"Is this you?"

I didn't know what to say!

"Carol, it's her. Look at her. She's shaking." Vice Principal Maximoff did not have my back.

"I know it looks like me, but I don't remember doing that, or being here. Tippy-Toe, do you remember this?"

"Chirruk, chirruk, chirruk."

"She doesn't remember, either! When was this?"

"This was last night, Squirrel Girl. You understand that . . . this looks bad. Can you tell us where you were at 9 P.M. last night?"

DOREEN'S NOTES

And the scariest thing? I don't remember! Tippy and I have no idea where we were! It's just a blank. I came from school, had dinner with my parents, and then the next thing I remember is waking up this morning.

But all I could do was tell the truth, so I did. But I had no proof and they just shook their heads.

"I didn't do this, though! I would never! Tippy-Toe and I love this school!"

And then Principal Danvers said the <u>worst thing ever</u>.

"I'm sorry, Squirrel Girl, but until we figure out what's going on, who did this, and where these posts came from, we have to suspend you."

NANCY: I'm so mad it's making me typo omg.

DOREEN: He wouldn't! AND, Nova says he never went to that bathroom, so he doesn't know where that picture came from.

NANCY: Oh, we are going to fix this. Or my name isn't Nancy Whitehead.

DOREEN: AND IT IS!

CHAPTER 8

OHIDH
(Overheard in Doreen's House)

MOM: Did you see the way Doreen walked in here, Dorian?

DAD: She looked so sad, Maureen. Our little girl has something going on and she doesn't want to talk to us about it.

MOM: I bet it's a super hero thing.

DAD: It is definitely a super hero thing! I wish she'd give it up. I don't understand why she puts herself through this.

MOM: It's too much for kids! Those super heroes shouldn't even be allowed to open a school. It's so dangerous.

DAD: And she doesn't have time to just hang out and have fun. So busy fighting Beembots and Eagles!

MOM: I think you mean Doombots and Vulture, dear.

DAD: Even worse!

MOM: I know, I know. We'll talk to her in the morning.

DOREEN: On top of all of this my mom and dad are gonna tell me not to be a hero tomorrow.

NANCY: What're you gonna do?

DOREEN: I . . . think I might write them a letter and leave it for them in the morning. And then come meet you so we can figure out how to fix everything.

NANCY: I think that is an A+ idea,

Dear Mom and Dad,

I think it's time I tell you what I love about being a super hero. When I was little, well, little-r, you told me that if we can, we should always help people. And you were right!

Being a hero means I get to help people all the time and that people will look to me for help. They'll see me, and they'll know that I'll be there for them.

I love that.

I was born with special powers that make it easier for me to, well, kick bad guys' butts than most people. Being a hero makes me feel more like . . . well, me! If I stopped, if I just quit, I think I'd stop being me. Or at least, the me that I like. I'd be someone different, but I'm happy with who I am. I hope you can be, too.

I love you!

Doreen
    (Dorian + Maureen = Doreen 4ever!!)

CHAPTER 9

TO: Squirrel Girl <squirrelgirl@heatmail.com>

FROM: no one <no0ne@n0thing.com>

Subject: Quit

You thought I wouldn't notice your snooping online? Looking for clues? Your friend left digital fingerprints all over everything! Ever heard of an IP address? Quit trying to find me. I'm way better at finding people than you. If you don't stop, everyone will see this video.

ATTACHMENTS

lookatwhatyoudid.mov

TO: Nancy Whitehead <catfannan@heatmail.com>

FROM: Squirrel Girl <squirrelgirl@heatmail.com>

Subject: Fwd: Quit

LOOK AT WHAT THIS JERK SENT TO MY SQUIRREL GIRL ACCT.

I AM ON MY WAY OVER AND I AM VERY MAD. THINK THEY CAN BLACKMAIL ME? I THINK NOT.

I PULLED THE LOCATION DATA AND IT WAS SENT FROM INSIDE THE SCHOOL.

Forwarded message

TO: Squirrel Girl <squirrelgirl@heatmail.com>

FROM: no one <no0ne@n0thing.com>

Subject: Quit

You thought I wouldn't notice your snooping online? Looking for clues? Your friend left digital fingerprints all over everything! Ever heard of an IP address? Quit trying to find me. I'm way better at finding people than you. If you don't stop, everyone will see this video.

ATTACHMENTS

lookatwhatyoudid.mov

TO: Squirrel Girl <squirrelgirl@heatmail.com>

FROM: Nancy Whitehead <catfannan@heatmail.com>

Subject: Fwd: Quit

OMG WE ARE GONNA GET THIS JERK!!

Also, okay, I analyzed that video and look what I found!!!

☑ As Ant-Man: Tell kids to look out for themselves, sow discord.

☑ As Rocket: Teach kids that they can walk away from a crime, make them lazy.

☑ As Amadeus: Pretend to cheat, get kicked out of school, take away the student studying dimensions!!

☐ DEAL WITH SQUIRREL GIRL—TOO NOSY

If it was YOU, why would you carry around a piece of paper that says you need to be dealt with? And I can't believe this person just . . . brought that paper with them. Did they think we don't know how to use video editing tools? lol.

Someone is out to get you and they are gonna RUE THE DAY.

CHAPTER 10

Ms. Marvel's List of Reasons Why That Was Definitely Not Ant-Man

1) He didn't make a single bad joke—actually, he didn't make ANY jokes!!

2) No smiles?? Not one???

3) He had no idea who Evan was, which was really weird. Like, literally he said, "Hello, young sir, may I have the pleasure?" and in what world would Ant-Man say "Hello, young sir"????

4) His hair was combed, there was no helmet hair to be seen. Super weird.

5) . . . Okay and most importantly, he told us to "take Squirrel Girl down."

ANT-MAN WOULD NEVER.

Squirrel Girl was right. There is something really wrong going on.

SG goes to bed at like 10 P.M. There's no way she'd be awake for this. —Miles

WHERE IS TIPPY????? —Evan

DOREEN WOULD NEVER LEAVE TIPPY-TOE BEHIND!
—Miles

123

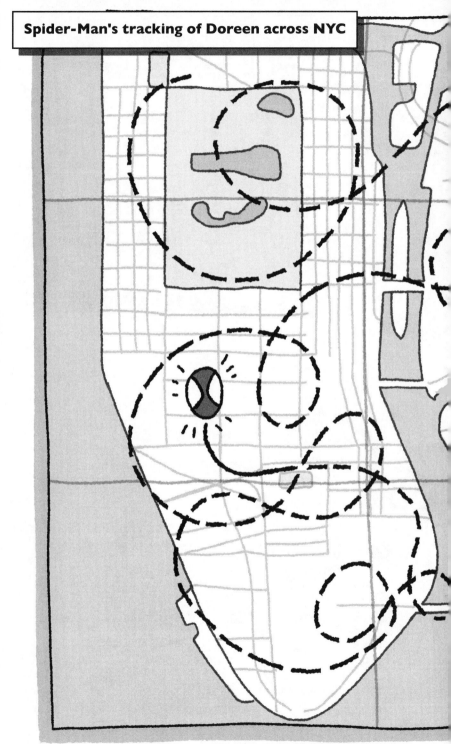

Spider-Man's tracking of Doreen across NYC

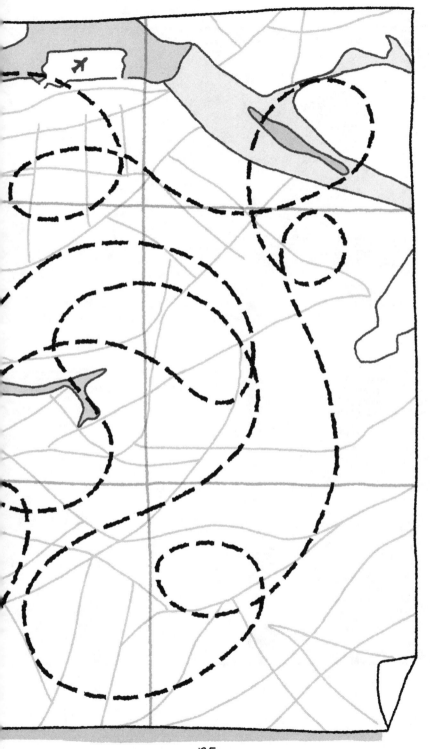

CHAPTER II

AVENGERS INSTITUTE
TRANSMISSION RECORD

MS. MARVEL: Hello? Hello??? Spidey??? Squirrel Girl???

bzztzzzbzzztttbzzztttt

NANCY: Doreen???? Ms. Marvel, do you have a visual???

MS. MARVEL: No! I'm still blocks away at the old Avengers Tower! Evan?

EVAN: No dice! I got stuck behind a group of tourists!

MS. MARVEL: Wait, I see . . . that can't be right. There's . . . Doreen's like ten feet away from me.

NANCY: What? How?

MS. MARVEL: . . . I don't think this is actually Doreen. She's . . . bullying some kid.

EVAN: What?

MS. MARVEL: She . . . just pushed some kid down and took his hot dog . . . This isn't Doreen. It's *Fauxreen.*

EVAN: Does she have Tippy-Toe??

MS. MARVEL: No Tippy-Toe!!

NANCY: A FAUXREEN FOR SURE.

MS. MARVEL: Okay, Evan, Nancy, meet me on the corner of Forty-Ninth and Ninth. We are gonna catch Fauxreen today.

EVAN: Already on the way, boss!

NANCY: I'll be there in five minutes, but I'm, uh, not a super hero, so feel free to do the fighting part without me.

MS. MARVEL: Right, right, yes! Take your time. Evan and I will chase her.

PLAN A: FOLLOW UP ON LEADS TO CATCH FAUXREEN

. . . uh, don't think we have any leads?

Spider-censor data is all corrupt. The trail just ends at the exact spot we disappeared. (Texted other Spider-Man but haven't heard back. It's possible he's in space.)

PLAN A:

PLAN B: ASK A TEACHER FOR HELP

How do we know who's a real teacher and who is an impersonator???

Spidey brings up a good point ^^

PLAN B:

PLAN C: COME UP WITH PASSCODES SO WE ALWAYS KNOW THE OTHER PERSON IS REALLY WHO THEY SAY THEY ARE

Mine is "one chorizo torta with extra avocado."

Mine is "live long and may the Force be with you."

Mine's "Saturday mornings are for cartoons."

Mine's . . . "hold on I want to think of a nut pun."

Mine's "I wish Thor was a giant cat."

Cool, we're all super dorky.

PLAN C: SUCCESS

PLAN D: EMAIL EVERY HERO WHO HAS DEALT WITH GOING TO ANOTHER DIMENSION

Email sent to Nightcrawler, Cloak, Blink, Thor, and Magik!

And I think they all went to spam because no one answered us. Maybe we should have bcc'd.

PLAN D:

PLAN E: REACH OUT TO OTHER KIDS AT SCHOOL TO SEE IF THEY'VE HAD ANY WEIRD STUFF HAPPENING ON THEIR TEAMS.

I'll message Amadeus. I know he's still suspended, too, so that'll be my opening line.

And I can talk to Nova.

I'll ask Moon Girl and Patriot and America! She can punch through dimensions!

I'll ask Ironheart. She might know something from working on the school newspaper!

PLAN E:

Kamala's Innermost Thoughts,
Hands Off!

I talked to Nova! Turns out some weird stuff is definitely going on. He's got the same gaps in his memory as Squirrel Girl, and he talked about something that went down after an Action Sequence class. And here is the wildest part . . .

Nova had a conversation with Rocket . . . and no Groot.

NO GROOT!

That is the most suspicious.

MILES'S NOTES

Okay, so Moon Girl was <u>not</u> interested in whatever I was bringing to the table. She said, and I quote, "I am in the middle of seventeen experiments, one of which is for the current Avengers team. I do not have time for whatever plot is going on inside this school. I'm sure you've got it. But if you're really stuck after exhausting all other leads, I guess you can come ask me again." And then she shut the door in my face.

America was helpful—she doesn't know specifics about what's going on, but she helped test the Spider-Tracer. And it turns out the versions I have don't do interdimensional travel well. Which is good to know.

(Would have been great to know three days ago, but you know, you live, you learn! Note to self: Tell the other Spider-Man we need to update these little dudes.)

Patriot, on the other hand, had plenty to say. He is also missing time, and his friends are all super mad at him. Apparently, they think he sold them out to one of his villains in exchange for becoming more powerful? But he swears he has no idea what they're talking about.

Evan's Journal KEEP OUT

Ironheart has also been suspecting something! She knew Squirrel Girl would never do something like that <u>and</u> that Amadeus Cho would never cheat, so she's been investigating on her own. She gave me all her notes and it looks like it's what we thought—the people who have been impersonated are:

Patriot

Nova

Squirrel Girl

Ant-Man

Rocket

. . . and probably Brawn—I think Squirrel Girl's talking to him now.

DOREEN'S NOTES

Amadeus and I have stuff in common turns out.

I messaged him and we decided to meet in the park near my house. He was already sitting on my favorite bench when I got there, and he started talking before I even sat down.

"So, you figured out someone's taking our places?"

"How'd you know??" I shouldn't have been surprised. He's probably one of the smartest people in the world.

"It wasn't that hard to figure out. I would never cheat, but that picture wasn't doctored. So, it had to be someone taking my place. And you'd never hurt the school; you love it too much."

"Yeah, there's definitely someone doing it, and when he takes our place, he takes us to another dimension."

DOREEN'S NOTES

That got Amadeus's attention.

"What??"

"Yeah, apparently it's this place where we don't remember anything. Spider-Man was with me the last time it happened, and I guess since he wasn't being body-copied, he could remember everything. I don't actually remember any of it."

"How do you know I'm me right now?"

". . . Hmm. Good question."

He grinned and stretched his arms over his head.

"You know it's me because no fake Brawn would be this perfect. There's always one thing wrong with a copy. But just in case, ask me about something that happened before all this started."

DOREEN'S NOTES

"What did you guys place in the decathlon last semester?"

He rolled his eyes.

"Second place, don't remind me. It's all because they made us fight fourteen dinosaurs."

"Fourteen?! We only had to fight two."

"What?!"

And then he started laughing. I put my hand on his shoulder. He seemed like he needed it.

"We're gonna catch this copycat, Amadeus."

He put one of his giant green hands on mine.

"I know we are. Okay, tell me about your plan."

DOREEN'S NOTES

Amadeus is in! I told him about the plan to follow everyone who might be our evil blackmailing villain.

PLAN F: Tail all the people who have been impersonated. Eventually one of them will become a faux version and then we quietly trail them and figure out who they are.

The "faux" works for almost everyone, omg.

Faux-va

Faux-reen

Faux-lk

Faux-triot

Fauxnt-Man

Oh, wait, never mind.

PLAN F: PENDING

SPIDEY'S POV

143

MS. MARVEL'S POV

EVAN'S POV

THIS IS DEFINITELY NOVA.
HE'S MAILING THE LETTERS
ONE BY ONE. IT'S WEIRD, BUT
NOT EVIL WEIRD.

NANCY'S POV

NANCY'S POV

CHAPTER 12

DO NOT OPEN
SPACE PHANTOM'S NOTEBOOK
I'M WARNING YOU
DON'T OPEN THIS UNLESS YOU ARE SPACE PHANTOM

Day 1:

Goals: • Take out Earth's super heroes
       • Rule Earth

Brainstorm

Go after Avengers

pros: Take out the big boys

cons: They are the big boys

Try to take an X-Man's place forever?

pros: Live in that beautiful mansion

cons: • How to stop being the X-Man and take
         over the world?
       • Can't some of the X-Men read minds? Too
         easy to be found out?

Avengers Institute!! Children!!

pros: I can defeat children! And it will take little
to no preparation. They're children, how hard
could it be?

cons: Captain Marvel is in charge but distracted
because she's doing two jobs

Day 8:

Ideas for new space in pocket dimension:
Color scheme: red and white cubes???
Cube-shaped things???

Day 13:

Some potential lives to take over:
Scott Lang AKA Bug-Man
Pietro Maximoff AKA Fast-Man

These two would be ideal. Scott is a disaster, and
Pietro is already in a leadership position. I worry
about the eyes Pietro always has on him, though.

There's also the big dog, JockLaw. Or maybe I'll
become Thor! Ha! The Space Phantom as the
Mighty Thor! Son of Oddus!

Day 20:

Have successfully infiltrated the school. Rocket Raccoon and Scott Lang were perfect covers. His tree friend Groot sleeps like a log and barely registers if Rocket leaves at night. Scott is so flaky he never realizes he's been gone! It's wonderful. I've started sowing the seeds of discord among the students and staff. They've already started fighting among themselves.

Day 25:

There are two students who are getting too nosy about things that matter to me: Squirrel Girl and that new Hulk. I need to get rid of them.

Day 30:

Success! They've been suspended and will no longer be an issue for me. Ha ha! I, Space Phantom, am on my way to world domination.

Slothbaby:
. . . How . . . how did this guy do anything? His information is . . . all wrong.

BRWN:
I'm embarrassed for all of us. He did no research.

CatFanNan:
. . . I'm not even a super hero or villain and I knew that notebook was bogus.

SEVAN_06:
I might actually be speechless.

AcornLuvr:
Maybe he was just too busy to write down the right things?

W3bbed4Life:
Sure, maybe that's it. Or maybe he's a bad super villain and that's why he went after *kids*.

BRWN:
ding ding ding

AcornLuvr:
I think I have an idea of how to
fix this, but I'll need your help,
Amadeus. I mean, well, I'll need
everyone's help, but first Amadeus.

Slothbaby:
Are we being replaced? 😊

AcornLuvr:
NEVER!!!!! Nancy, you too. You and
Amadeus are part one of the new
Plan to End All Plans!

W3bbed4Life:
I am ready for the Plan to End All
Plans. I'm so embarrassed that this
guy who clearly did no preparation
for his evil doings was so hard
to find. I need this to be over
fast. And we will never speak of
it again.

154

DOREEN: Okay, Amadeus's password is "I am Brawn"

MILES: lol cool

EVAN: So we're phase 2?

KAMALA: Got the notes on phase 1—but

DOREEN: BUT

MILES: Why is there always a "but"?

EVAN: lolololol

KAMALA: still funny

DOREEN: lol guys! okay! BUT because of the way the machine is set up, the code can't make it work any quicker than what it's built to do. It's going to take at least 90 seconds to actually create our own pocket bubble dimension around this Space Phantom person. Our job is to make that minute and a half pass without the Space Phantom knowing what's going on. We're meeting them at Amadeus's lab.

KAMALA: As my dad says: easy-peasy lemon cheesy, my friends.

MILES: No way your dad says that.

KAMALA: 🙂

CHAPTER 13

162

CHAPTER 14

TO: Avengers Institute Students
   <avengers-student-list-serv@avengers-institute.com>

FROM: Carol Danvers <cdanvers@avengers-institute.com>

Subject: An apology and a congratulations

Dear students,

We're sending out a school-wide email to recognize the unfair punishment and innocence of Squirrel Girl and Amadeus Cho (as well as Nova, who, I am told, did not use that restroom). Both Squirrel Girl and Amadeus Cho have been cleared because it was, in fact, the Space Phantom who was on our campus impersonating your friends and our fellow staff members. But alongside Ms. Marvel, Spider-Man, Evan Sabahnur, as well as a civilian friend, Squirrel Girl and Amadeus helped to subdue and imprison Space Phantom and we are once again clear and safe.

In addition, we will be redoing both Ant-Man's independent study and Rocket and Groot's Action Sequence classes next semester as they fell prey to Space Phantom's body swapping. Ethics and Tools of the Super Hero Trade shall go on as scheduled.

Col. Carol Danvers
Principal, Avengers Institute

DOREEN'S NOTES

All's well that ends well?

Everyone at school is congratulating us, but when I asked Principal Danvers how we'd stop this from happening again, she just shook her head and said she was going to talk to Doctor Strange about it . . . Although maybe that means next semester we'll get to learn MAGIC!!

And one of the most important things happened after I got home.

My parents were waiting for me, and my dad was holding the letter I left them, and the first thing they did when I walked in was hug me and tell me how proud they were of me for my letter. They were so sorry for pressuring me into being anything I don't want to be. Then we all cried a lot. Tippy-Toe did not appreciate how many tears were dried with her bow, though. I'll have to get her a new one.

DOREEN'S NOTES

Home with the parents and feeling way better!

Our daughter, the super hero

Okay! Since we are doing OPERATION CELEBRATE BEATING AN EVIL SPACE PHANTOM SLUMBER PARTY, we can officially move on from super hero drama. Tell me EVERYTHING I HAVE MISSED in the Land of Nan.

Honestly, the best thing is getting one-on-one time with my BFF ... like, celebrating with your super friends tomorrow will be fun, but this is for us. And now I will tell you about what Mr. Dorsett said about his mom in Engineering last week and you are going to *die* because it was so RUDE.

Doreen's Super Friends Scrapbook

OPERATION CELEBRATE BEATING AN EVIL
SPACE PHANTOM (continued)

(by hanging out and being Kids for a day)

Nothing like flying Kites and playing
cards at the beach!

Two seconds after this, a seagull stole Evan's hot dog.

But we got him another one!

Don't ask me how we all fit back here for this picture!!

New. Best. Day. Ever.

DOREEN: Um . . . did anyone else just get a packet today???

MILES: Uh, yeah and hand delivered by Professor Maximoff

KAMALA: Is this for real???

EVAN: I don't know if I should be excited or scared

DOREEN: BOTH MAYBE??

MILES: Definitely both. Wolverine freaks me out.

Xavier's School for Gifted Youngsters
1407 Graymalkin Lane
Salem Center, New York

Dear Squirrel Girl,

We are thrilled to x-tend an invitation to you to attend

a semester of classes at the Xavier Academy in

Westchester. We've sent similar invitations to several

of your classmates, so you'll be attending alongside

friends and colleagues. Please find all relevant details

in the attached welcome packet. Our students are

x-cited to meet you all.

Cordially yours,

Professor Charles Xavier

DOREEN'S NOTES

OMG! Training with mutants???
SIGN ME UP!

Me OMW to Xavier Academy

PREETI CHHIBBER has written for SYFY, Book Riot, Book Riot Comics, The Nerds of Color, and The Mary Sue. She has work in the anthology *A Thousand Beginnings and Endings*, a collection of retellings of fairy tales and myths, and is the author of the *Spider-Man: Far from Home* tie-in *Peter and Ned's Ultimate Travel Journal* for Marvel. She hosts the podcasts *Desi Geek Girls* and *Strong Female Characters* (SYFY Wire) and has appeared on several panels at New York Comic Con, San Diego Comic-Con, and on-screen on the SYFY Network.

JAMES LANCETT is a London-based illustrator, director, and yellow sock lover! As a child growing up in Cardiff, Wales, he was obsessed with cartoons, video games, and all things fantasy. As he grew up and became a lot more beardy, these inspirations held strong and so he moved to London to study illustration and animation at Kingston University. This degree opened the door to a job he had dreamed of ever since he was a kid and he now works as an illustrator and animation director.